The Very St
Turkey

Story by
Katharine Kenah

Pictures by
Binny Talib

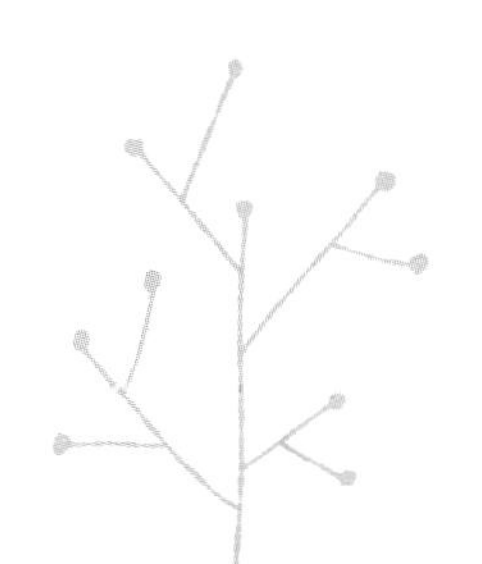

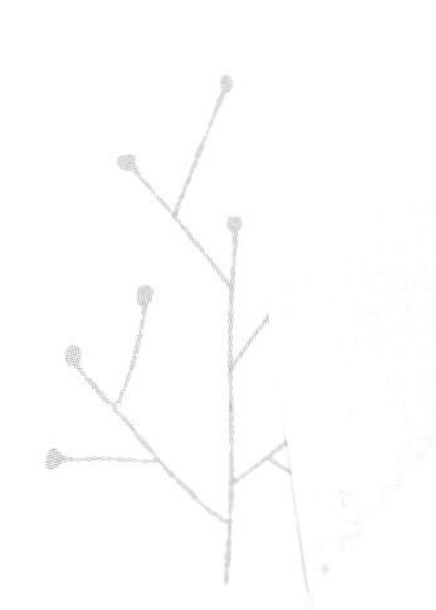

Cartwheel Books
An imprint of Scholastic Inc.

For Sarah, Sam, Eli,
Christy, and Benjamin,
with much love

—KK

To my beautiful family
(none of whom are turkeys),
my constant inspiration

—BT

Library of Congress Cataloging-in-Publication Data available
ISBN 978-0-545-76109-3
10 9 8 7 6 5 4 16 17 18 19
Printed in the U.S.A. 40
First edition, September 2015
Book design by Leslie Mechanic

To: Turkey
Turkey's House
To: Turkey's
House
5¢

It was Thanksgiving morning and Turkey had a problem. Pig, Horse, Goat and Sheep, Cow, and Mouse had each invited him to Thanksgiving dinner at their homes. Turkey loved his barnyard friends and didn't want to hurt anyone's feelings. He was going to *everyone's* house!

Turkey wasn't sure he had room in his stomach for five dinners. But then he thought of all the good food bubbling and baking in those kitchens. Just thinking about it made him hungry!

Five houses. Five dinners. No problem!

It was time to get ready.

Turkey hopped up and down,

and touched his beak to
the ground twenty-five times
to stretch his stomach.

He brushed his feathers.

Then Turkey made a map of the way to his friends' houses.

He was ready to go!

Turkey walked to Pig's house first. Pig was outside hanging up holiday lights. The piglets were playing pumpkin ball nearby.

"Hi, Turkey," said Pig. "Hope you're hungry."

One of the piglets made an amazing pumpkin pass that almost hit Turkey's head.

"Touchdown!" called Turkey as he caught the ball and kicked it back to the piglets.

"Half time!" yelled Pig. He climbed down the ladder and waved everyone into the house for dinner.

Pig made a fine Thanksgiving stew
with beets and corn and a worm or two.

While Pig's family snuffled and snorted, Turkey slurped and burped. He gobbled up everything on his plate!

Turkey felt like part of the family. It was a **wonderful** feeling.

Horse's house was next. Turkey wished he hadn't eaten like a pig when he saw the dining room table. It was covered with plates of oat cakes and hay, carrots, sugar cubes, and pumpkin and apple pies.

While Horse's family munched and crunched, Turkey mashed and mixed. He gobbled up everything on his plate!

"I have an idea," Horse said after dinner. "Let's have a race."

Turkey didn't think that was a good idea. He was too full to trot, and his tummy was feeling funny.

While Horse's family raced ahead, Turkey hopped and fluttered behind them. But he didn't get too far, so Horse gave Turkey a ride under fall leaves as colorful as candy.

Turkey felt like part of the family. It was a **wonderful** feeling.

Goat and Sheep lived next door to Horse.
Turkey sniffed the air all the way to their house.

"What is that yummy smell?"
Turkey asked as he waddled through
their front door.

"Come see," they said.

Goat made his special Thanksgiving soup, with flowers, weeds, and glue. Sheep baked a clover casserole dotted with dandelions. While Goat and Sheep tasted and sipped, Turkey gobbled up everything on his plate!

"That soup was sticky," said Sheep.

"Dandelions taste fuzzy," said Goat.

Turkey said, "Dinner was delightful!" But he thought he might explode.

They played hide-and-seek indoors after dinner.

Goat and Sheep
kept peeking,

but Turkey won every time.

Turkey felt like part of the family. It was a **wonderful** feeling.

Turkey was too late for dinner when he got to Cow's house. They were getting ready for dessert. Cow's family was crowded around the kitchen counter. They were all holding spoons and ice cream cones. There were cartons of ice cream everywhere . . . in so many flavors it looked like a rainbow!

"Ready?" asked Cow. She handed Turkey a cone and spoon.

"For what?" Turkey said.

"Our family's Thanksgiving ice cream cone contest," said Cow. "The tallest cone wins. Ready . . . set . . . GO!"

Ice cream flew through the air. Everyone was shouting, pushing, and laughing. The kitchen was a mess!

Turkey felt like part of the family. It was a **wonderful** feeling.

Turkey had one house left to go—Mouse's.

When he got there, the table was crowded with mothers and fathers, sisters and brothers, grandparents, cousins, uncles and aunts.

"Happy Thanksgiving, Turkey!" they shouted.

Dinner was a feast of birdseed, soap, and berries. While Mouse's family went nibble, nibble . . . taste, taste, Turkey gobbled up everything on his plate!

"Now comes the best part," said Mouse.

"What?" asked Turkey. He hoped it wasn't ice cream.

"Our family's Thanksgiving parade," said Mouse.

They put on their coats and boots, blew up balloons, and handed a drum to Turkey. Turkey was so full he thought they could use *him* as a balloon. A gigantic floating Turkey!

When everyone was ready, the Mouse family parade marched out the door with Turkey at the front of their long, noisy line.

Turkey felt like part of the family. It was a **wonderful** feeling.

Neighbors poured out of their homes to join the parade. Turkey saw Pig. He saw Horse. He saw Goat and Sheep. He even saw Cow. He saw every one of his barnyard friends.

Turkey was so happy,

so surprised,

and so *stuffed*,
he fell over!

When Turkey opened his eyes, his barnyard friends were in a circle around him, looking at him with worried faces.

"How do you feel?" asked Horse.

"I ate too much," said Turkey. "But it was worth it. I got to spend Thanksgiving with *all* of you. And that's what families do."

"Sorry, Turkey," said Cow. "We didn't know we *each* invited you to dinner."

"That's okay," said Turkey. "But next year we're having Thanksgiving dinner at *my* house!"

Everyone laughed and cheered. It was a **wonderful** feeling.

The parade started again. While Turkey banged his drum, he planned what to make his barnyard family for dinner next year. Grilled grasshoppers were always good. Just thinking about it made him hungry!